HEIDI

HEIDI

JOHANNA SPYRI

Retold by
Susan Saunders

Illustrated by
Jada Rowland

Troll Associates

Library of Congress Cataloging-in-Publication Data

Saunders, Susan.
   Heidi / by Johanna Spyri; adapted by Susan Saunders; illustrated
  by Jada Rowland.
     p.   cm.
   Summary: A Swiss orphan is heartbroken when she must leave her
beloved grandfather and their happy home in the mountains to go to
school and to care for an invalid girl in the city.
   ISBN 0-8167-1215-8 (lib. bdg.)   ISBN 0-8167-1216-6 (pbk.)
    [1. Grandfathers—Fiction. 2. Mountain life—Fiction.
3. Orphans—Fiction. 4. Switzerland—Fiction.] I. Rowland, Jada,
ill. II. Spyri, Johanna, 1827-1901. Heidi. III. Title.
PZ7.S2577He 1988
[Fic]—dc19   87-15466
                                     CIP

10   9   8   7   6   5   4   3   2   1

On a clear, sunny day in June, Heidi and her Aunt Dete climbed the narrow path leading from the valley to the top of the mountain. Heidi was a slender little girl with curly dark hair and brown eyes. She was wearing two dresses and a shawl—all the clothes she owned—one on top of the other. The day was warm, so Heidi's cheeks were even rosier than usual.

Halfway up the mountain, on the other side of the village of Dorfli, Dete met an old friend. They walked together for a time, leaving Heidi to explore the mountainside while they talked.

"Where are you taking the girl?" the woman asked Dete. "She is your sister's child, isn't she—the orphan?"

"Yes. Both of her parents are dead, and I can no longer care for her," Aunt Dete replied. "I am going to Frankfurt to work, and I'm taking Heidi up the mountain to live with her grandfather."

"Her grandfather!" the friend exclaimed in surprise. "The few times a year he comes down from the mountain to Dorfli, he frightens everyone in the village with his glaring eyes and enormous beard! And he never speaks to anybody."

"But he is Heidi's grandfather, and he must look after her now," Dete said firmly.

"The poor child!" said her friend. "I have always wondered why the grandfather lives as he does, all alone in a hut on top of the mountain."

"I will tell you." But first Dete looked around for Heidi, because she didn't want the little girl to overhear.

"There she is," said her friend, "scrambling up the slope with Peter the goatherd and his goats."

Aunt Dete lowered her voice. "When he was young, Heidi's grandfather was the owner of one of the finest farms in Domleschg valley," she told her friend. "But he was a gambler, and lost his farm and all his money. Soon after that, he disappeared—some say he became a soldier—and his old parents died of sorrow.

"When he returned to Domleschg fifteen years later, he had a small boy with him—his son, Tobias. But no one in the valley would have anything to do with him or Tobias. Furious, he brought the boy to Dorfli to live."

"What became of Tobias?" her friend asked eagerly.

"Tobias learned to be a carpenter, and he married my sister, Adelheid. Heidi is their child," Dete went on. "But Tobias was killed by a falling beam while he was building a house. My sister became ill from the shock of his death and died only two weeks later."

"I'm sorry," said her friend. "Tell me about the grandfather."

"People began to say that he had brought about their deaths by leading such a wicked life when he was young. So the grandfather moved to the hut on the mountain and never came down."

The friend stopped at the shack where eleven-year-old Peter the goatherd lived with his mother and old grandmother. Dete said goodbye and walked farther up the path, looking around for Heidi.

The little girl and Peter were taking their time climbing up the mountain, as Peter's goats stopped here and there to eat especially tasty plants. Peter sprang nimbly from rock to rock in his bare feet. But Heidi was clumsy and hot in all of her clothes. Suddenly she sat down and pulled off her thick shoes and stockings. Next came the heavy wool shawl and her Sunday dress. Last, Heidi unhooked her dress and laid it on top of the pile of clothes. Barefooted and wearing only a light woolen slip, she could move as easily as Peter now.

"Heidi, what have you done with your clothes?" Aunt Dete screamed when she saw her niece.

"They're down there," Heidi said, pointing calmly down the mountain.

"Careless good-for-nothing!" Aunt Dete scolded. "What made you undress yourself?"

"I don't want any clothes," Heidi answered.

But Aunt Dete sent Peter back for Heidi's things. Then Aunt Dete, Heidi, and Peter and his goats followed the steep path up the mountain to the grandfather's hut. On a wooden seat outside was the grandfather himself.

Peter walked off with the goats, but Heidi marched straight up to the old man, put her hand out, and said, "Hello, Grandfather."

9

"What is the meaning of this?" he said gruffly, staring at Heidi from under his bushy gray eyebrows.

"I have brought you Tobias and Adelheid's daughter," Aunt Dete told him. "I have done my duty by her for four years. Now it is your turn."

"What am I to do with her?" the grandfather growled.

"Do with her as you like," Aunt Dete answered. "I have work waiting for me in Frankfurt."

The grandfather rose from his seat. "Off with you, then!" he thundered. "Do not let me see your face here again."

And Aunt Dete left in a hurry. The old man sat back down, lost in thought. Heidi put her hands behind her back and gazed at her grandfather without speaking.

"What is it you want?" he asked her at last.

"To see what you have inside the house," Heidi replied.

"Come, then," the grandfather said, leading her into the hut.

Inside there was a table, a chair, a cupboard—and her grandfather's bed in one corner.

"Where shall I sleep?" Heidi asked.

"Wherever you like," he answered, seeming not to care.

Heidi chose the hayloft, which had a round window overlooking the valley below. With an old sheet from the cupboard and an extra heap of hay for a pillow, Heidi was content.

A shrill whistle woke her early the next morning. Heidi climbed quickly down the short ladder from the hayloft and ran outside. There she found Peter with his flock, and her grandfather with his two goats.

"What are their names?" she asked him.

"The white goat is Little Swan, and the brown one Little Bear," her grandfather replied. "Would you like to go with Peter and the flock up the mountain?"

Heidi would like nothing better. Overhead, the sky was a deep blue, and the sun shone brightly on huge meadows of blue and yellow flowers. Heidi had never felt so happy in her life.

Peter and Heidi spent the whole day on the mountain-side. Heidi learned the names of each of the goats: Little Snowflake, Great Turk, and Greenfinch. She shared the food her grandfather had packed with Peter, who never really had enough to eat. She picked a cluster of flowers. The whole day, she ran and skipped and played.

As the sun set, turning the slopes red and gold, Heidi and Peter started back down the mountain.

"Come with me again tomorrow!" Peter said when
he delivered Heidi and Little Swan and Little Bear
to her grandfather.

Heidi spent day after day with Peter and his flock until she
was strong and tanned and healthy. Soon the summer
passed, and autumn came. The wind blew louder and
stronger through the three old fir trees next to her grandfather's hut.

Sometimes the old man would say, "Today you must stay at home, Heidi. A sudden gust of wind could blow you over the rocks and into the valley." When she did stay at home, Peter was sad. He knew his day on the mountain would be long and dull without Heidi to keep him company. But Heidi amused herself by watching her grandfather build furniture or make cheese from goats' milk.

Autumn gave way to winter, and it grew very cold. Snow covered the mountain. Peter did not come with his goats, since there wasn't a blade of grass for them to eat. The days grew lonely for Heidi.

Then one afternoon there was a thump on the door of her grandfather's hut. It was Peter, all covered with snow. He had come to visit them. When he sat next to the warm fire, the snow melted, turning him into a tiny waterfall.

"Now that it's winter, you must turn to your pen and pencil," the grandfather said with a smile to Peter.

"Why must he do that?" Heidi wanted to know.

"Peter must go to school to learn to read and write," her grandfather replied.

Peter nodded, although he wasn't very happy about it. Peter had a hard time putting his thoughts into words, so school was very difficult for him. He still hadn't learned to read.

Heidi and her grandfather shared a meal with the boy, who enjoyed every bite. He thanked them and promised to come again in a week. As he was leaving, he added, "Heidi, my grandmother would like you to visit her."

Heidi had never been invited to anyone's house for a visit before. It was an exciting idea. When she woke up the next morning, she told her grandfather, "I must go down to see Peter's grandmother today. She will be looking for me."

"The snow is much too deep," said her grandfather.

But Heidi asked again and again. A few days later, the old man agreed. He brought Heidi's cover down from her bed in the hayloft. He wrapped Heidi in it, then sat with her on a big wooden sled. They went down the mountainside on the sled so fast that Heidi thought they were flying!

Outside Peter's hut, her grandfather said, "When it begins to grow dark, you must start home. I'll come back for you then."

17

Heidi waved good-bye and opened the door. She walked through the kitchen, which was a dark little room with a fireplace and a few dishes, and into a second small room. Peter's mother sat at a low table, patching one of his jackets. In the corner was a much older woman, spinning wool at a spinning wheel. Heidi went straight over to her and said, "Grandmother, I have come at last."

The old woman reached for Heidi's hand. "Are you the child who lives up on the mountain? Are you Heidi?"

"I am," Heidi said. "My grandfather just brought me here on his sled."

"What is she like, Brigitte?" the old woman asked Peter's mother.

"She is slender, like Adelheid," Brigitte answered. "But she has dark, curly hair, like her father, Tobias."

18

Heidi had been looking around the small, dark room. Suddenly she exclaimed, "One of your shutters is banging in the wind. It should be nailed shut! Do you see it, Grandmother?"

"I hear the shutter, and many other rattles and creaks as well. This old house is falling to pieces," Peter's grandmother answered. "But I can see nothing, dear child."

"I'll take you outside, then," Heidi told her, "into the bright light of the sun. Then you can see."

Peter's grandmother shook her head. "It will never be light for me again on this earth—ever." It was then Heidi realized the old woman was blind.

Heidi burst into tears. She cried so hard for the old woman who couldn't see that at last the grandmother said, "Come, Heidi, let me listen to you talk. It is such a joy for me to hear a kind word."

So Heidi dried her eyes and began to tell about her happy life with her grandfather. The afternoon passed quickly. As the sun sank behind the mountain, Heidi's grandfather returned to carry her back home through the deep drifts.

"Tomorrow," she told him, "we must go to the grandmother's house and fasten the shutter. We must also drive in many more nails in other places to stop the rattles and creaks. And can you make it light for her, Grandfather, so she can see?"

The grandfather looked at Heidi for a while without speaking. Finally he said, "At least we can stop the rattling, Heidi. We will mend the hut, starting tomorrow."

Heidi's grandfather returned with her the next day and made the hut strong and tight. Heidi herself visited Peter's grandmother almost every day. The grandmother felt the darkness much less when Heidi was with her. "I hope the child is never taken from me," she said.

19

So the winter passed, then a summer with Peter and the goats, and then another winter. Heidi was now eight years old, and the March sun was melting the snow on the mountainside when a visitor arrived at the grandfather's house. It was Heidi's Aunt Dete, wearing a long dress and a fine feathered hat.

The old man looked at her. He didn't trust her. But Dete ignored the hard look he gave her, and said what she had come prepared to say. "A rich man in Frankfurt, Mr. Sesemann by name, has an only daughter who can't walk. She's in a wheelchair, and her mother is dead. The girl would like a playmate because she is very lonely."

"What does this have to do with us?" the grandfather interrupted.

"I will tell you," said Dete sternly. "Heidi is my sister's child. I am responsible for what happens to her. She is now eight years old, and she knows nothing." Dete was clearly angry. "You haven't sent her to school, not even to church. In Frankfurt, she will share the daughter's lessons and have all sorts of good things. This is a lucky chance for Heidi, and

there is not one person who wouldn't agree with me. If you interfere, I'll have you brought to court!"

"Take the child and be gone then!" roared the old man. "I never want to see you again!" And he stamped out of the hut.

"I'm not coming with you," Heidi said firmly to her aunt.

"Nonsense!" said Dete. "Do you want to be as stupid as one of the goats?"

As Dete dragged her down the mountain, Heidi could hear the old grandmother calling from her hut: "Dete! Do not take the child away from us!"

Dete and Heidi left for Frankfurt that very evening. They traveled all night and part of the next day by train. It was in the late afternoon that Dete rang the bell at the Sesemanns' house.

Dete and Heidi were taken upstairs to speak to Miss Rottenmeier. She was the housekeeper, and she watched over Mr. Sesemann's daughter, Klara, while he traveled on business.

Miss Rottenmeier frowned down at Heidi in her ragged dress and old straw hat. "What is your name?"

"Heidi," replied the child.

"What kind of name is that?" asked the woman sternly.

"If the lady will allow me, I will speak for the child," Dete said. "She's not used to strangers. Her real name is Adelheid, for her mother."

"That's better," Miss Rottenmeier sniffed. "But she is so young. I had expected a child closer to twelve, Klara's age."

"Heidi is ten, or thereabouts," Dete mumbled.

But Heidi spoke right up. "Grandfather told me I was eight," she said, ignoring Dete's finger, which was poking at her back.

"Only eight!" exclaimed Miss Rottenmeier. "What books have you studied?"

"None," said Heidi.

"Then how did you learn to read?" asked Miss Rottenmeier.

"I have never learned to read, or Peter either," Heidi answered truthfully.

"How could you bring me such a child!" Miss Rottenmeier complained to Dete.

"I am late. I must go now," Dete said hurriedly. "I will come again soon to see how she is getting along." She rushed downstairs and out the front door before Miss Rottenmeier could catch her.

Klara had been watching from her wheelchair in the hall. She had a pale, thin face and bright blue eyes that seemed friendly. "Come here," she said to Heidi. "Would you rather be called Adelheid or Heidi?"

"I'm always called Heidi," she replied.

"Then Heidi will be your name," said Klara.

Later at supper, Miss Rottenmeier told Heidi how she must behave at the table, when to go to bed, when to get up, how to keep her room neat, and so many other things that Heidi's eyes began to close.

When she finally came to the end of her list of rules, Miss Rottenmeier said, "You must remember all that I've told you, Adelheid. Have you understood everything?"

"Heidi has been asleep for a long time," said Klara with a smile. Dinner hadn't been so entertaining in ages, she thought.

When Heidi opened her eyes the next morning, she didn't know where she was at first. She saw long white curtains, two big chairs, a sofa—not her warm little bed in the hay at her grandfather's. All too soon, she remembered she was in Frankfurt. Heidi leaped from the bed and dressed herself. She ran from one window to another, trying to see the sky and the countryside.

To her disappointment, she saw only buildings. She pushed at the windows of her room, but she couldn't open them. Heidi was frightened, like a bird in a cage. But she felt a little better at breakfast when Klara told her the servants would open the windows for her.

Then Klara's teacher arrived. He tried to teach Heidi her ABC's, but she found it hard to pay attention to the pages of little black marks. She rushed to the window because a passing cart had sounded like the wind in the fir trees back home. Or one of the letters reminded her of a goat's horn, and she would have to tell Klara about Little Swan.

As the days passed, the teacher worried that Heidi would never learn to read. But Klara was happy. With Heidi nearby, Klara felt more alive than she had before. And she thought less and less about why she couldn't walk. Even the usually dull study hours went by quickly when Heidi was there.

Often Heidi would sit beside Klara and tell her stories of the mountain—of the goats, and the three fir trees, and her grandfather, and Peter and his grandmother. But sometimes Heidi would get so homesick that she would cry out: "I have to go home! I have to go now!"

Klara would quiet her. They must wait until Mr. Sesemann came home, Klara said. He would know what to do.

Finally, Mr. Sesemann returned from his business trip. He went straight to his daughter's room, where Klara was sitting in her wheelchair with Heidi close by. Klara greeted her father with great tenderness. She loved him dearly, and he loved her. Then Mr. Sesemann held out his hand to Heidi, who had retreated into a corner of the room.

"Tell me, are you and Klara good friends?" he asked kindly. "Or do you argue and get cross, then cry and make up, and then begin all over again?"

"No, Klara is always good to me," Heidi answered shyly.

"And Heidi never tries to quarrel," added Klara quickly.

Miss Rottenmeier, of course, told a different story. "Sometimes," she said, "Adelheid does such peculiar things that she doesn't seem to be in her right mind!"

But Mr. Sesemann could see with his own eyes that Klara was happier than she had been in years. "So you don't want me to send the child home again?" he asked his daughter. "You aren't tired of having her here?"

"Please don't, Papa," Klara pleaded. "Time passes so much faster since Heidi came. Something new happens every day, and she has so much to tell me."

"Then she will stay with us for as long as you like," said her father.

Mr. Sesemann soon had to leave again on business, but Klara's grandmother arrived for a visit. She had beautiful white hair and such a kindhearted expression that Heidi liked her immediately.

She had brought Heidi some books as a present, but Miss Rottenmeier shook her head. "What can the child do with books? She hasn't even learned her ABC's!"

"Heidi doesn't look like a child who can't learn the alphabet," said Grandmother Sesemann.

The little girl opened her eyes wide when she saw the lovely pictures in the books. She was especially taken with one of a shepherd in a beautiful green pasture. It reminded her of Peter and his goats.

"How do you get along in the study hours with Klara's teacher?" Mrs. Sesemann asked.

"Not at all well," answered Heidi. "People can't learn to read—it's too hard."

"Where did you ever hear that?" Grandmother Sesemann asked, surprised.

"Peter told me," the little girl replied.

"Heidi, you will learn to read," said the grandmother. "As soon as you can read, you may have the book for your own, so that you can learn the whole story."

Heidi looked down at the picture and sighed. "Oh, if only I could read now!"

Not more than a week of Grandmother Sesemann's visit had passed when Klara's teacher asked to see her. "Something has happened that I never expected," he reported excitedly. "Heidi can read!"

"Many unexpected things happen in life," replied Mrs. Sesemann calmly.

For Klara and Heidi, the grandmother's visit was over too soon. The house seemed empty after she left, as though everything had come to an end. Heidi stopped telling Klara she wanted to go home because she didn't want to seem ungrateful. But Heidi longed to be with her grandfather on the mountain again. At night, she cried herself to sleep. During the day, she ate very little, growing thin and pale. As the weeks passed, Heidi felt sadder and sadder.

Suddenly a mystery disturbed the Sesemann house. One morning when the servants came downstairs, they found the front door standing wide open. Since the door had been locked carefully the night before, no one could understand how it had happened.

But it happened again, and then again. The servants began to talk of a ghostly figure in white that wandered the halls of the house. Miss Rottenmeier became so uneasy that she wrote to Klara's father, asking him to come home.

Mr. Sesemann thought the whole thing was silly. But he invited an old friend, Dr. Reboux, to keep him company while he waited up for the "ghost."

The two men made themselves comfortable in a room downstairs, talking quietly and waiting for the night to end.

Suddenly the doctor lifted his finger to his mouth. "Sssh. Don't you hear something?"

As they listened, the locks on the front door turned with a loud click. The big door was pushed open.

Picking up a candle, Mr. Sesemann stepped out into the hall, the doctor close behind him. "Who's there?" the doctor thundered.

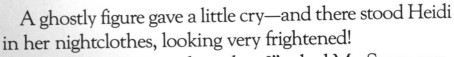

A ghostly figure gave a little cry—and there stood Heidi in her nightclothes, looking very frightened!

"Heidi, why are you down here?" asked Mr. Sesemann.

White with fear, Heidi stammered, "I—I don't know!"

Doctor Reboux stepped forward. "She walked in her sleep," he murmured. "Let me talk to her."

He took the trembling child upstairs to her room. "Now you tell me," he said gently, "where you wanted to go."

"I didn't want to go anywhere," Heidi answered. "But all of a sudden I was downstairs."

"Were you dreaming anything?"

"I always dream I'm with my grandfather," Heidi replied sadly. "I hear the wind in the fir trees. I open the door of the hut to see the sky and the stars . . . and then I wake up."

"Where did you live with your grandfather?" the doctor asked.

"Up on the mountain," Heidi answered.

"Isn't it rather dull there?" asked Doctor Reboux.

"No. It's lovely! So lovely!" Heidi burst into tears.

The doctor laid Heidi's head on her pillow. "Tomorrow, everything will be all right," he told her.

Downstairs, the doctor explained the situation to Mr. Sesemann. "The child is wasting away from homesickness. She's almost to the point where she's a ghost herself. There is only one way to cure her—send her back to her home on the mountain as soon as possible."

"It will be done at once," said Mr. Sesemann.

Very early the next morning, Mr. Sesemann woke Miss Rottenmeier and told her to pack a trunk for Heidi. Besides Heidi's own clothes, Mr. Sesemann told his housekeeper to pack many of Klara's clothes for the time when Heidi would grow into them. Then he spoke to his daughter. Klara was very upset at first because she didn't want Heidi to leave. But her father was firm. And he promised Klara that she could visit Heidi the following summer.

When told she was going home, Heidi could hardly believe it. But when she saw the trunk and a basket of soft rolls Klara had packed for Peter's old grandmother, Heidi jumped for joy. Before she knew it, she was on a train traveling back to the mountain she loved.

Heidi arrived home wearing a new hat and a beautiful new dress. She climbed up the steep path from the village as quickly as she could, stopping first at the house of Peter's grandmother.

"Is that you, Heidi?" the old woman cried. "Have you really come back to me?"

"Yes, I'm really here!" Heidi answered. "And I'm never going away again."

Heidi changed out of her fine dress and put on the old dress and hat she'd been carrying with her. "So Grandfather will recognize me," she explained, smoothing out the creases with her hands. Heidi then kissed Peter's grandmother good-bye and continued up the mountain.

It wasn't long before she saw the tops of the three fir trees above the roof of the hut, then the hut itself, and finally her grandfather! He was sitting outside, smoking his pipe just as he had in the old days. Heidi rushed up to him and threw her arms around his neck.

For the first time in many years, the grandfather's eyes filled with tears. Then he put Heidi on his knee and gazed at her for a moment. "So you have come home, Heidi," he said, wiping away a tear. "But you don't look like a grand lady. What happened? Did they send you away?"

"Oh, no, Grandfather," Heidi answered. "You mustn't think that. They were all so good—Klara and her grandmother, and Mr. Sesemann. But Grandfather, I couldn't bear to wait any longer to come home to you."

Suddenly, a shrill whistle pierced the still mountain air. Heidi stepped around the hut to see where the whistle came from. Soon a whole flock of goats appeared, leaping down from the heights, with Peter in the middle of them. When he saw Heidi, he stood perfectly still and stared at her, speechless.

"Good evening, Peter," Heidi called out. "Don't you know me?"

The goats must have recognized her voice because they rubbed their heads against her, bleating with joy as she called them by name.

When Heidi stepped back inside the hut, she found her bed had already been made up. The fresh straw smelled wonderful. That night, Heidi slept deeply, peacefully, something she hadn't done the whole year she was in Frankfurt.

Time passed swiftly for Heidi. Soon she was as tanned—and her cheeks as rosy—as she had been before leaving the mountain. Heidi spent her days happily. She climbed the steep mountain slopes with Peter and the goats, helped her grandfather with the chores, and read stories to the old grandmother. When winter came, Heidi went to school in the village with Peter.

It was during a bright day in early summer, however, that a strange procession of people made their way up the mountain from the village. Closer and closer they came. Heidi could soon see two men carrying a chair on which a young girl sat, wrapped in shawls. Behind them were a grand lady on a horse, a small boy pushing an empty wheelchair, and finally a man with more shawls and cloaks piled in a basket on his back.

Heidi ran to get her grandfather. Jumping up and down in excitement, Heidi could barely get the words out. "Grandfather, they're here! Klara and her grandmother!"

39

No sooner did the procession arrive in front of the hut than Heidi rushed over to Klara. The two friends hugged each other, tears of joy welling in their eyes.

After getting off her horse, Grandmother Sesemann walked over to the grandfather and exclaimed, "What a splendid place you have! Many a king might envy you!"

Klara was equally enchanted. "How beautiful it is here!" she said, her eyes gleaming. "I'd like to stay forever!"

Heidi helped Klara get into her wheelchair and then

pushed it around the hut. She showed Klara the fir trees and all the blossoming flowers on the slope of the mountain. Afterward, the grandfather served a delicious meal of freshly baked bread and cheese. The hours flew by, and it seemed Klara and her grandmother had only just arrived when it was time for them to go.

"The sun is starting to set. The men will be returning to take us back down the mountain," the grandmother said.

"I have been thinking," said Heidi's grandfather slowly. "If you agree, we might keep Klara with us for a while. I'm sure it would do her good."

"You are indeed kind," Klara's grandmother replied. "I was just thinking myself that a stay on the mountain would be the very thing for her!"

Heidi and Klara looked at each other and shrieked with happiness!

The next morning, both girls woke up early. The grandfather helped Klara into her wheelchair, then pushed it out into the sunshine. The pure mountain breeze was so cool and refreshing that every breath was a pleasure. The grandfather brought two bowls of foaming, snow-white milk from Little Swan and handed one bowl to Klara and one to Heidi.

Soon Peter came by with his flock. But when he asked Heidi to come with him up the mountain, she said, "I won't be able to come while Klara is here with me."

Peter scowled at the girl in the wheelchair. He was jealous!

Klara grew stronger and healthier on the mountain. She slept well, and she ate more. And each day the grandfather asked her to try to stand for a minute or two.

Finally, the grandfather decided that Klara was strong enough for a day on the higher slopes where the goats grazed. He pushed the empty wheelchair outside. Then he walked into the hut to help the two girls get ready for the trip.

At just that moment, Peter happened to pass the hut. He glared at the chair like an enemy. It belonged to Klara, and Klara had taken Heidi from him. If I get rid of the chair, he thought to himself, then the girl will have to go back where she came from. Peter glanced quickly around, then shoved the chair down the mountain! He scampered away before it crashed on the rocks far below.

"It must have been the wind," Heidi decided when they couldn't find the chair outside the hut.

"Now we won't be able to go up the mountain," Klara added sadly.

But the old grandfather was stubborn, and he carried Klara up the mountain in his arms. He left the two girls on the slope until evening, with Peter's goats playing above.

Heidi and Klara sat happily together for hours. Then Heidi climbed a little higher to look for a field of flowers she had seen the year before. When she came back, she exclaimed, "You must come, Klara! The flowers are more beautiful than you can imagine — thousands of them in blue, yellow, and gold. I'll carry you!"

"You're smaller than I am, Heidi," Klara pointed out. "You can't carry me. Oh, if only I could walk!"

Heidi tried to think of a plan. Then she looked up at Peter above them. "Peter, please come down here and help us," she called.

She asked Peter to get hold of Klara on one side while she held the girl on the other. The two of them were able to lift Klara up. Then Klara tried to use her feet a little. "Just press down," Heidi suggested. "I'm sure it will hurt less."

Klara tried. She took one hesitant step forward. It made her cry out. Still, she lifted her other foot and put it down too.

"Do it once more," Heidi urged eagerly.

Klara did, and it was a little easier than before. "Heidi, I can take steps!" Klara exclaimed.

Heidi was beside herself with delight. "Now we can come up here together every day and go wherever we like. And you will get quite strong and well!"

Even Peter was thrilled that his rival for Heidi might really be able to walk again.

When the grandfather came up the mountain for them, Heidi rushed to tell him the news. Then he lifted Klara up, put his arm around her, and Klara walked!

Not long after that, Klara's grandmother wrote to say exactly when she was coming. Again a procession of people climbed the mountain from the village, with the grandmother in the lead on her horse. She looked up at her granddaughter, sitting outside the hut with Heidi. "Klara, is it you?" she called out. "Your cheeks are as red as apples!"

Then Heidi stood up, Klara quickly leaned on her shoulders, and the two friends started walking together.

The grandmother jumped down from her horse and ran to them. Laughing and crying, she hugged Klara, then Heidi, and then Klara again. Suddenly she caught sight of Heidi's grandfather.

"It is your work!" she said. "It is your care and nursing...."

"It is the good sun and the mountain air," said the old grandfather with a smile.

"I must telegraph my son to join us," Klara's grandmother said. "I won't tell him why. It will be the greatest joy of his life!"

Mr. Sesemann arrived the very next week. When he saw Klara healthy and walking, he wept with happiness. He gathered his daughter in his arms and hugged her tightly. Then to Heidi's grandfather he said, "You will understand me when I tell you that for many long years I have had no real happiness. What was all my wealth when I looked at my poor, sick child? How can I ever repay you?"

"Mr. Sesemann, I have already been well rewarded. I have Heidi back with me, and I have seen your daughter walk." The grandfather paused. "But I do have one wish."

"Name it, old friend," urged Mr. Sesemann.

The grandfather spoke softly so he couldn't be overheard. "I am old. When I go, I cannot leave the child anything. If you would promise me that Heidi will never have to earn her living among strangers..."

"I give you my hand on it!" Mr. Sesemann said quickly. The old man shook Mr. Sesemann's outstretched hand. They were both smiling.

The following morning, packed and ready to go, Klara started to cry as she said good-bye. But Heidi comforted her. "Next summer, we will go out every day with Peter and the goats, and climb to where the flowers grow, and enjoy ourselves every moment." Klara stopped her sniffling.

Heidi and her grandfather waved as Mr. Sesemann, the grandmother, and Klara—no longer needing her chair—descended the mountain. Heidi held her grandfather's hand as the procession disappeared from view. In her heart, Heidi knew Klara and she would always remain good friends. And soon they'd be together again on the mountain they both loved.